Evie's Magic Bracelet

Read more in the Evie's Magic Bracelet series!

Evie's Magic Bracelet

The Unicorn's Foal

JESSICA ENNIS-HILL
and Elen Caldecott

Illustrated by
Erica-Jane Waters

Hodder
Children's
Books

HODDER CHILDREN'S BOOKS

First published in Great Britain in 2017 by Hodder and Stoughton

1 3 5 7 9 10 8 6 4 2

Text and illustrations copyright © Jessica Ennis Limited, 2017

The moral right of the author has been asserted.

A CIP catalogue record for this book
is available from the British Library.

ISBN 978 1 444 93442 7

Printed and bound in Great Britain
by Clays Ltd, St Ives plc

The paper and board used in this book
are made from wood from responsible sources

Hodder Children's Books
An imprint of
Hachette Children's Group
Part of Hodder and Stoughton
Carmelite House
50 Victoria Embankment
London EC4Y 0DZ

An Hachette UK Company
www.hachette.co.uk

www.hachettechildrens.co.uk

To Carmel x
– J.E-H.

To Ed and Thalia
with love
– E.C.

Chapter 1

Evie Hall fizzed inside with excitement. The air around her fizzed too with bursts of gold magic because Evie was so delighted.

It was snowing outside. Really snowing!

She was tucked up inside, early in the morning. She was snuggled up warm on a big armchair in the window, watching the flakes fall and the magic sparkle. There was always magic in the air whenever anyone was happy, or joyful, or excited. She was able to see it because of a gift from a unicorn. Sometimes she could even use the magic to make all kinds of brilliant-and-amazing things happen, but only when she was wearing one of Grandma Iris' bracelets.

It had been a really long time since a new bracelet had arrived. Weeks and weeks and weeks! She was beginning to wonder whether Grandma Iris had forgotten about her, or changed her mind about sharing magic.

But the snow was too brilliant for Evie to stay worried for long.

'Look, Luna!' Evie said. 'It's going to be a white Christmas!'

Luna, the cat, wasn't fond of the cold, or the wet, and only liked Christmas because of the baubles on the tree; she liked to hunt them down when no one was looking. Luna yawned, before curling into a comfier position on Evie's lap.

No one else was awake in the house and the street outside was quiet. The settling white snow made it seem like the world was tucked up under a duvet. It was beautiful. Evie stroked Luna and watched the rising sun cast glistening shades of peach and pink and gold across the ice.

'I wonder if Mum would let me go and play out before breakfast if I promise to wrap up warm?' Evie said to Luna, who purred a happy reply. Evie rubbed between Luna's ears in the way that the cat really loved. 'It's Christmas in four days, Luna. I've asked Mum and Dad for a new bike. Do you think I'll get it?' Luna purred even louder. Evie took that as a good sign.

4

It was just then that she saw movement out on the street. Someone was walking towards her house, a tall someone dressed in red, carrying a heavy sack. She felt a little leap in her heart, then giggled to herself. No. It wasn't Father Christmas! There were still three more sleeps until he would be visiting. It was the postman, crunching his way towards their front door.

Evie sat up, and Luna leapt to the floor with a yowl. 'Sorry, Luna, but he's coming this way!' Evie said. She rushed into the hall and fumbled with the lock and snib. As soon as she opened the front door, swirls of cold air whipped into the house.

'Morning, Evie,' the postie said, 'I've got

something for you today.'

For her? She tried to squish down her eagerness – it probably wasn't from Grandma Iris. It might even be something horrible like a letter from school reminding her to do her holiday homework.

But then, she saw the box that the postie pulled from his bag. It was square, with red and white wrapping, and her name and address written on it in curly, dancing handwriting – Grandma Iris' writing!

Hurray!

'Oh thank you, thank you,' she said, taking the gift from the postie.

'You're welcome. Better get back inside, it's colder than a polar bear's eyebrows

6

out here.' The postie trudged back to the street, leaving deep footprints in the snow as he went.

Evie shut the door and rushed back to the warmth of the front room. Grandma Iris hadn't forgotten her, she'd just been saving up the magic. The parcel was tied with ribbon, so Evie unwrapped it gently. Beneath the ribbon and paper was a box. She lifted the lid.

It was a bracelet.

She felt her insides shiver with glee.

The bracelet was made of clear crystal beads, each one so small and delicate that she could hardly see where one bead stopped and the next one began. Evie lifted it and slid it on to her wrist.

Every bracelet that Grandma Iris sent
worked a different kind of magic. Since
the bracelets started arriving she'd used all
kinds of magic: she'd been able to speak to
animals, she'd brought objects to life, and
she'd even conjured things from thin air.
What could this bracelet do? She touched
the beads with the tip of her finger.

Then, she looked inside the box again.
Grandma Iris liked to leave puzzles that
hinted at the magic she'd been sent. They
didn't usually help much, as the puzzles were
tricksy! But maybe this time Grandma Iris
had been clear, like the beads. There was a
slim slip of card, with the puzzle carefully

printed on it. Evie read:

> *Look through me and you will find*
> *Magic of a different kind.*
> *Three turns, three days is all you get.*
> *Can you see the answer yet?*

Evie had to grin. Grandma Iris was talking in riddles as much as ever. There were a few things she did understand in the rhyme now that she'd had a few bracelets. The magic would begin to work when she turned it three times, and it would run out after three days. But the rest of the puzzle was a mystery.

She listened carefully to see if the rest of

her family was awake yet. All she could hear was the soft clang of water in the heating pipes. Mum and Dad were still asleep, with Myla the dog curled up in her bed in the corner of their room. And Lily, Evie's little sister, was in her room too.

It was just her and Luna.

It was the absolute perfect time to try out her new bracelet.

Evie Hall,
6 Javelin Street,

She twisted it three times around her wrist. A band of gold light flowed out of it, like water from a tap. It twisted around her hand, around her arm, up and across her body.

As the magic wrapped itself around her, Evie realised that she couldn't see her wrist any more, or her hand. She flexed her fingers in panic. She could still feel them, they were still there, she just couldn't see them!

Her arm vanished, then her belly.

The light twirled around her legs – they disappeared.

Evie rushed over to the mirror that hung above the fireplace. It was decorated with tinsel. She could see the bright green holly Mum had added too.

But she couldn't see herself. Where her face and shoulders should be, there was absolutely nothing.

She patted her face. She could still feel her nose and her mouth and her cheeks. But they weren't in the mirror, it just reflected the room behind her.

The new bracelet made her invisible.

'Would you look at that?' she asked Luna.

But Luna flicked her tail back and forth angrily – where had her comfy seat and stroke gone?

Evie laughed. 'Well, I guess that means you can't.'

Her voice echoed in the front room. But her body was nowhere to be seen.

This was going to be fun.

Chapter 2

A completely invisible Evie stood in the middle of the front room. Luna stalked from the armchair to the settee, hunting for her missing mistress.

She mewed loudly.

Evie reached down to pet the cat's fur and Luna leapt in surprise. Her tail pointed straight up in the air, like an angry exclamation mark. Evie picked Luna up and cuddled her. Luna mewed again, but soon seemed to decide that feeling Evie was good enough, even if she couldn't see her. Luna settled into the cuddle.

'Sorry, Luna.' Evie giggled. 'I didn't mean to frighten you.' Evie carried Luna back to the armchair and put her in the seat carefully.

She was the first one awake and she was invisible. Her mind raced with all the things she might do. She could go and make Lily believe her room was haunted, flying her dolls through the air and whispering 'woooo' near her ear.

It was tempting. Very tempting. Lily could be very annoying sometimes.

'Or what about some nice treats?' she asked the cat, who was licking her paws. Evie might go next door to Nana Em and Grandpa's and raid their goodies cupboard – Mum was a nurse and would only let them eat sweets at weekends. But Nana Em had a cupboard filled to the brim with chocolate and biscuits. An invisible visitor might be able to do some secret snacking without getting caught.

Or she could call her friends Isabelle and Ryan and see what they'd like to do with the power of invisibility – they always shared her magical adventures.

Evie could have danced with excitement at all the possibilities.

So she did. A lot.

Once she was done with the twist and jazz hands and the air guitar, she flopped down on the settee, out of breath.

It was still snowing outside. Fairy lights

on the house opposite blinked and winked. They made the shape of an electric reindeer on the front wall, flickering red and green and yellow, saying Christmas is on its way!

And that was when Evie realised what she most wanted to do with her brand new power.

Somewhere in the house was the big present she'd be getting for Christmas from Mum and Dad. She'd been asking and asking for a new bike; her old was too little now, it was more Lily's size than Evie's. She'd seen a brand new nine-speed bike in the window of the cycle shop that she'd fallen in love with. And gone on about a fair bit too.

'What do you think, Luna? Mum's worried about me riding in the road outside. And Dad said bikes were expensive. I mean, any present is nice, but a bike would be so lovely.' She hopped across the room and dropped down in front of Luna. 'If I get a bike, I can get a basket and you can ride around with me. Would you like that?'

She had no idea whether she'd be getting her ultimate, dream present. If she stayed silent, and was super careful, maybe she could find out.

She was pretty sure that Mum and Dad would be hiding their gifts in their bedroom. It was the biggest room in the house and she and Lily didn't go inside very often. It also

had an enormous wardrobe, big enough
to hide an elephant in – if you had
an elephant on the run and it needed
somewhere to lie low.

'Should I?' she asked Luna. 'It won't do
anyone any harm. And I really, really, really
want to know.'

Luna didn't reply.

Evie felt as though there were two Evies
inside her: one saying that she should go and
look, to put her curiosity to rest; the other
Evie saying no, it was a bad idea and would
ruin Mum and Dad's surprise.

Curious Evie won out.

Evie headed from the front room and
padded up the stairs, careful not to make

them creak. She edged along the landing to Mum and Dad's bedroom.

The door was ajar. Mum liked to be able to hear the girls if they got up in the night. Evie could see Myla, the dog, curled up in her bed on the floor. Mum and Dad were two lumps hidden by their squishy duvet. The room was gloomy, with the only light coming from Lily's night-light on the landing.

Evie pushed the door open wide enough to be able to slip inside. Myla's head jerked up at the sound, but, when she couldn't spot any danger, she dropped it back down again.

Evie crept further into the dark room. The wardrobe was on her left, in the corner.

It was huge and loomed in the shadows. Rats! The wardrobe door was closed. She was going to have to sneak closer and—

'Morning.'

Evie froze. Mum had spoken. Mum had seen her! Her heart pounded in her throat.

'Morning, Anna,' Dad's voice replied.

Evie breathed again. Mum and Dad were just talking to each other. They hadn't spotted her. She held her hand up in front of her face. Nothing. She was still invisible. Phew.

'Is it time to get up?' Mum whispered.

'No, it's still the middle of the night.'

'No, sorry, love, it's definitely morning. However much you wish it wasn't.'

Evie saw Mum throw back the duvet and tuck her feet into her slippers. She walked across the room in her pyjamas and drew the curtains. 'Snow!' Mum said.

Evie stayed as still as a statue. She was never going to be able to complete her mission with Mum and Dad awake. This was a disaster!

'It snowed?' Dad sat up, his hair stuck up in all directions. 'Does that mean you won't have to go to work today?'

Mum sighed and looked out. 'No. It means it's going to be hard to get to work. But I have to go.'

If Dad got up too, all hope was lost. She'd never get to peek inside the wardrobe.

Worse, they might even bump into her, and discover she was invisible. And then she'd have a heap of explaining to do. Evie took some gentle, delicate paces back towards the landing.

Myla yawned and stretched in her bed.

'I'll get on with breakfast while you take the first shower,' Dad said. 'And we really have to tell the girls today.'

'I know.' Mum sounded sad.

Tell the girls what? Evie stopped moving again. Was someone ill? Was it Mum or Dad or Nana Em?

'I'll hate not being here on Christmas Day,' Mum said softly, looking out the window. 'It's horrible.'

Mum wasn't going to be home on Christmas Day? Evie felt the news settle like frost in the pit of her stomach. Where was she going to be? This was awful.

'I know,' Dad said. 'We'll miss you. But the hospital needs you too. And think of the money!'

Mum was going to work on Christmas Day? She wouldn't be there to see what Father Christmas brought? Or to open her own presents? Or to play board games or snuggle on the settee in front of Christmas films? Evie felt a lump form in her throat. A sob.

But she couldn't make a noise when she was inside the room, she just couldn't.

She squashed it back down.

She stepped backwards. She was near the door. One last step. She was out.

Out on the landing, away from the bedroom door, she turned her bracelet three times. Gold light flowed from it and as the light wrapped itself around her wrist, she could see her skin again, then the cuff of her dressing gown, then her arm. Soon her whole body was back where it was supposed to be.

But all the excitement of the snow and Grandma Iris' present was gone. There wasn't a single speck of magic to be seen.

Mum wouldn't be there when they woke on Christmas Day. She'd be spending the day at work. Worse, Dad had said they had to think of the money. Evie felt a stab of guilt. She'd been asking for a new bike for weeks and weeks, even though she knew how expensive they were. It was her fault Mum was going to be working.

Christmas was officially ruined.

Chapter 3

Evie could hear everyone else getting up
and getting dressed and getting in each
other's way in the bathroom. She was sitting
downstairs, at the table, trying not to feel sad.

Mum wasn't going to be home for
Christmas. She was going to be at work
earning money for bikes.

Myla the dog clattered into the room, bustling around her feet in a waggy-good-morning way.

But even that wasn't enough to cheer Evie up.

'Coo-ee! It's only me,' Nana Em called from the kitchen. A draught of cold air whirled in, as Nana Em came through the back door. 'Hello, pet,' Nana Em said, planting an icy kiss on Evie's forehead. 'Are you all on your tod? Where is everyone?'

Evie planted her chin in her cupped palms and rested her elbows on the table. 'I got up really early, because I heard the snow whoomph down the roof. Everyone else is upstairs.'

'Yes! Snow!' Nana Em clapped her hands

together. She was wearing mittens so it
made more of a *fuff* noise than a clap. 'I
love the snow, don't you? It turns everything
to Wonderland. Or Narnia. Or maybe the
North Pole. Magical, anyway.'

'Hmm,' Evie said.

33

Nana Em pulled out a chair and sat down. Evie noticed her wellies with fur around the top and her puffy white coat and bobble hat. She was really dressed for the weather.

'What's up with you?' Nana Em asked. 'Aren't you excited about the snow?'

'I suppose.'

'Well, you could have fooled me. I've seen more enthusiasm in wilted cabbage.'

Evie shrugged. She couldn't tell Nana Em about Mum. If she did, she'd have to admit she'd been listening in on Mum and Dad's conversation, and she was bound to be in trouble for that.

'Well,' Nana Em grinned, 'I've come over to invite you two girls to celebrate the snow with me. I've sent your grandpa to the shed to dig out our old sledge. There's a hill in Beau Mount Park that's just brilliant for sledging. What do you say?'

Evie shrugged again. She got down from the table and went into the kitchen. Luna meowed loudly next to her bowl. Evie dumped some biscuits for her. Then she put a slice of bread in the toaster.

Nana Em appeared in the doorway. 'Come on, Evie. Imagine it. Shooting down the old hill at a rate of knots with the wind in your hair and frost in the air. Isabelle and Ryan can come too. Doesn't that sound fun?'

It did.

A bit.

The toast popped. 'I'll just eat this then find some wellies,' Evie said.

'Excellent!'

The park was already busy by the time they got there. Evie and Lily, Grandpa and Nana Em who dragged the sledge behind her. Evie had called Isabelle and Ryan, they were on their way too.

They walked through the gate, past the copse of trees where Evie had seen a unicorn last summer, towards the big hill. There was thick snow and people whizzed down on sledges, and tea trays and even bin bags. Bright flashes of gold magic streaked through the air behind the people. A whole troop of snowmen stood to attention around the hill, watching the activity with their coal eyes. Beyond the hill a snowball battle was in full swing in front of the café, and Evie could hear the whoops and yells of the fighters.

'Bagsie first down the hill!' Nana Em said as magic bloomed above her. She raced up the bank, puffing hard and tugging her boots free from the deep snow.

'Ooph,' Grandpa said, trudging behind her, 'I'd rather a nice day out at the railway museum, or the old ironworks, but your Nana has a knack for getting her own way.' He and Lily did their best to keep up.

37

But Evie dragged her feet. She made deep channels in the snow with her wellies. She just couldn't stop thinking about Mum, at work, on Christmas Day.

'Come on, slowcoach!' Nana Em called to her.

The others were right at the top of the hill, ready to sledge down.

Evie tried to run, but slipped and landed – *whoomph* – in a snow drift. 'Yuck!' Icy drips ran down her sleeves. A couple of people who'd seen what had happened, laughed.

Evie wished she could just disappear.

And then she remembered that she could! All she had to do was twist the bracelet on

her wrist and she'd be invisible.

She scrambled to her feet as fast as she could. Perhaps the day wouldn't be so bad after all. Not if she could use magic to bring some fun to it.

Isabelle and Ryan were on their way, and it would be perfect to meet them with a magical surprise … and perhaps a sneaky snowball or two?

'Nana Em, is it all right if I go and wait for Isabelle and Ryan and play with them for a bit?' she yelled up at Nana Em.

'OK!' Nana Em waved. 'But be back in time for snacks at elevenses!' Then, 'Wheee!' she set off down the slope, bobble hat bobbing.

Evie ran back towards the gate and
ducked into the copse of trees. There was a
prickly hawthorn thicket that was perfect
for hiding from the view of the sledgers.
She turned her bracelet three times. Again,
the twisting gold magic hid her hands, her
wrists, then all of her was gone.

Evie giggled.

She weaved between the trees, so that

she wouldn't leave any telltale tracks, then, when she was near the gate, she started making snowballs. Lots of snowballs. She soon had a pyramid of ammunition at her feet and the gate in sight.

She was ready.

Chapter 4

Evie watched the gate intently. Isabelle and
Ryan would be through any minute. She and
her snowballs were ready for them.

There! Isabelle was first, wrapped up
warm in a puffy purple jacket and huge
woolly hat pulled over her dark hair. Ryan
followed behind, his hands pushed deep into

his pockets. Evie had to be patient, and wait for them to step into range. She passed a snowball from one hand to another.

Now! She threw her first ball and it exploded in a white cloud on Ryan's leg.

'Hey!' he yelled, and scooped up a snowball of his own. Then paused, as he

realised he couldn't see his attacker.

Evie giggled at the confused look on his face. Then she sent a second snowball after the first.

Ryan saw it coming and dodged out of its path at the last minute. 'Who's there?' he shouted.

A third snowball landed on Isabelle's welly boot. The fourth on Ryan's arm. He danced out of the way of her fifth. He spun about like a top, trying to see where the snowballs were coming from.

Evie covered her mouth with a cold hand, trying to squish down her laughter.

'Who's throwing them?' Isabelle called.

'I don't know,' Ryan said. 'It looks like no one!'

'It has to be someone,' Isabelle insisted.
'Snowballs don't fly by themselves, unless it's
by magic!'

Isabelle and Ryan looked at each other –
and broke into grins. They did know one
person who used magic. 'Evie!' Isabelle said.
'Evie, is that you?'

Evie crunched towards them, leaving a
trail of footprints behind her in the snow.
But that was the only sign that she was
even there.

'You're invisible,' Ryan laughed. He
reached out and patted the air, and finally
touched her shoulder. 'There you are!
Did you get a new bracelet from your
Grandma Iris?'

Evie nodded. Then she realised that there
was absolutely no point in nodding at all
– they couldn't see her! 'Yes,' she said. 'It
came this morning.'

'Wow,' Isabelle said, in wonder.

'Have you been having fun with it?'
Ryan asked.

For a moment, Evie felt a stab of sadness.
No, it hadn't been fun. She'd found out
that Mum was going to be working on
Christmas Day because she'd been asking
for a bike for so long.

Then she felt a shower of cold snowflakes
settling on her head – Ryan had thrown a
handful of snow in her direction.

'That is so cool,' he said.

'No,' Evie laughed, 'that was cold!' She
shook the snowy drips from her hat, then
she scooped a chunk of snow at Ryan.
He scooped back, and soon they were all
shrieking and whooping under showers of
snow and bursts of magic sparkles.

'You can't catch me,' Evie yelled in glee.
She turned away from the raucous battle
and ran. Isabelle and Ryan chased her
footprints, eager to keep up. She ducked and
spun and twisted to get away. But they were
gaining on her, laughing and shouting.

The trees! If she headed for the trees she
could hide in the patches that were sheltered
from snow. She headed for the copse again,
running as fast as she could, but trailing

telltale prints behind her.

'She's going that way!' Ryan yelled.

'After her!' Isabelle added.

In seconds, Evie was scrambling through a thicket, crawling under low branches, over bare earth. She wasn't leaving any prints now.

She heard Ryan and Isabelle pushing their way through too – twigs snapped and dry leaves rustled. Evie backed up against the thick trunk of a sycamore tree. The tree had no leaves, but its high branches had caught the snow and stopped it from settling on the ground. She pressed her palms into the bark and stood as still as she could, not making a single sound.

'Where is she?' Isabelle asked Ryan. She turned round in a circle, looking straight past Evie!

Evie pressed her lips tight together to smother her giggles. Isabelle looked cross and impressed and amused, all at the same time.

Ryan held up his hand. 'Hush! If we listen really carefully we might be able to hear her.'

Evie wanted to laugh so much, but if she did they would definitely catch her. Isabelle and Ryan were both as silent as sleeping statues. Evie was on tenterhooks.

'Ryan,' Isabelle said, 'we need to make her laugh. Why did the toilet roll roll down the hill?'

'I don't know, why did the toilet roll roll down the hill?'

'To get to the bottom.'

Evie shook with quiet giggles.

'How do you make an octopus laugh?' Ryan asked.

Isabelle turned her head, listening keenly. 'I don't know, Ryan, how do you make an octopus laugh?'

'With ten-tickles.'

Evie couldn't help it, she laughed out loud. Isabelle lunged towards the noise, arms outstretched, and caught Evie by the hands. 'Got her!' Isabelle said in triumph.

'Good work,' Ryan said.

Evie rested her hands on Isabelle's, still

laughing at the silly jokes. 'Fair enough, you got me,' she said.

She let go of Isabelle and twisted the bracelet on her wrist three times. Magic flowed out of it and soon they could both see her again.

'I can't believe bad jokes gave the game away,' Evie laughed.

'Can I have a turn too?' Isabelle asked.

'Of course.' Evie handed the bracelet to her friend. Soon they were playing hide and seek with one invisible player, which made it quite hard, but lots of fun. Ryan had a turn too, then it was back to Evie. Her giggles gave her away again.

She was just about to let Isabelle have

another go when she heard something that made her stop. A clattering, clopping noise. It sounded big, and heavy, and whatever it was was tearing through the undergrowth nearby, shaking branches and snapping twigs. Isabelle's eyes widened in fear.

'What is that?' she whispered.

'I don't know,' Ryan said, 'but it's big and it's headed our way. Hide!'

He grabbed Evie's wrist and pulled her down towards a fallen log with a tangle of ivy growing around it. Isabelle was right behind them. They crouched and waited for whatever it was to crash into the clearing.

Chapter
5

The crashing noise was getting closer
and closer. Something huge was tearing
through the trees. Snow flurries shook
down from the branches and birds flew
upwards in alarm.

Ryan, Isabelle and Evie were crouched
beside the fallen log, watching anxiously.

What could it be?

Then, the creature burst into the clearing and they could see who it was. The unicorn! It was the unicorn they had met on their very first magical adventure. He was tall, with a silvery coat and a shimmering pearl horn. Last time they had seen him, he had been friendly, but now he was stomping through the bushes, sweeping his horn angrily from side to side.

Isabelle stood up slowly. 'Hello?' she said, quite timidly for her.

The unicorn snorted and white puffs of cloud billowed from his nose. 'What?' he snapped.

'Hello,' Isabelle said again, a little more

boldly. Evie stood up, Ryan too. They all quaked under the unicorn's glare.

'Do you remember us?' Evie said. 'Grandma Iris gave us bracelets to do magic?'

The unicorn tossed his head and his white mane rippled. He looked so handsome, and so cross, both at the same time. 'I remember you. A unicorn never forgets. We're like elephants, but without the ridiculous noses.'

Evie stepped closer. The shredded leaves meant her footsteps made no sound. Still, she was careful not to make any sudden movements – she didn't want to annoy the unicorn any more than he was already. 'Is everything all right?' she asked.

'No,' the unicorn snapped. He pawed at the ground, crushing leaves.

'Can we help?' Ryan asked.

'What's the matter?' Isabelle added.

The unicorn looked left, then right, hardly able to stay still. 'It's my foal,' he said. 'He wanted to play in the snow. He loves snow. So, we came here. But he wandered away. My son, he's missing.'

The unicorn dropped his head and his ears pressed close to his mane. He looked so unhappy, Evie knew they had to do something.

'We'll help you find him,' Evie said with certainty.

'I've been looking for him for ages,'

the unicorn said scornfully. 'I've scoured the hill and the lake and the woods and I can't find him. What good will three children do? You'll just get in the way.'

Evie bristled. The unicorn was upset, but that was no reason to be rude! 'Four pairs of eyes have to be better than just one,' she said. 'Even if three of those pairs belong to humans.'

The unicorn snorted, then pawed the earth. 'I'm sorry,' he said finally, 'you're right. I didn't mean to be ungrateful. I'm just, well, I'm frightened.'

Evie strode closer and rested her hand on the unicorn's warm flank. 'It's all right,' she said. 'I understand. Mum gets nippy when she's worried too sometimes.'

The unicorn pressed up against her palm.

'Will we be able to see your foal?' Isabelle said doubtfully. 'I mean, what with him being a magical creature and everything?'

'Most people can't see us at all,' the unicorn said. 'But you've been touched by

unicorn magic, so that won't be a problem. He isn't invisible. He's missing.'

'Where did you see him last?' Ryan asked, all business-like.

'Earlier this morning,' the unicorn said. 'The first flurry of snow fell as the sun rose and it was so beautiful we came out to canter. We ran around the whole park three times, dodging in and out of the people, who couldn't see us at all. Then I stopped for a rest. I'm not as young as I used to be. And when I looked around there was no sign of him.'

'Where was this?' Isabelle pulled her woolly hat down firmly on her head – she was ready to start the search too.

'Near the adventure playground,' the unicorn said.

'Right.' Evie patted the unicorn one last time. 'We'll start there. Mum always says that if we get lost we should stay right where we are until she finds us.'

'Your mum sounds very sensible. But I've already looked all around there. Now the snow's been churned up by people there are no prints at all,' the unicorn replied.

Evie paused. She didn't want to waste time, but they had to start somewhere, and it seemed sensible to go to where the foal had last been seen. She made a decision. 'You carry on looking in the copse,' she told the unicorn. 'We'll go to the playground.

We can all meet up in thirty minutes back in this spot. Does that sound like a good idea?'

The unicorn nodded stiffly. 'Yes, thank you.'

They were all ready to head out of the trees towards the lake, when Isabelle paused. 'Wait,' she said. 'We don't know your foal's name.'

'He's called Arthur Shining Star Proudfoot Prancer the Third. He's named after me, Arthur Shining Star Proudfoot Prancer the Second. But we call him Junior for short.'

'Junior it is,' Isabelle said with a wink. 'Thanks, Mr Proudfoot Prancer the Second. Let's go!'

So the three friends left the woods,

ducking under branches and rustling
their way through leaves, until they were
out in the open and ready to search for the
lost foal.

Chapter
6

'Junior!' Isabelle yelled at the top of her voice.

'Hush!' Ryan said.

'Why? We're looking for him, aren't we?'

'Yes, but look.' He pointed to a group of children who were standing by the gate. They were all staring at Isabelle. 'We don't want to draw too much attention to ourselves. I mean, we can't tell the whole park we're looking for a lost unicorn, can we?'

It was a good point. They were going to have to be subtle. Careful. Cautious. Like a fox training to be the next James Bond.

'Junior!' Isabelle yelled again.

Evie rolled her eyes.

They had reached the adventure playground. There was a fence running around it, half buried in snow. Beyond the fence was a climbing wall with colourful plastic handgrips and a climbing frame that dangled red ropes as well as a rope web that stretched up towards the trees. The stumps

of wood that were meant for balancing
on were topped with blobs of white
snow, like ice cream cones. There was no
sign of Junior.

Evie looked out at the park. She could see
the frozen lake in the distance, with skaters
twirling figures of eight. Closer to the
adventure playground, two boys bashed at
frozen puddles with stones, sending chips of
ice up into the air.

'We should look for hoofprints,' Evie
said firmly. 'Junior might have left a trail
we can follow.'

The other two nodded and they all
stepped through the gate. The play park
was quiet, with only a few climbers and

clamberers. But it had been used a lot
already. Dozens of footprints, boot prints
and welly prints covered every inch of snow.
There were too many to be able to spot
Junior's hooves.

'It's no good,' Isabelle said after ten
minutes of looking. 'There have just been

too many visitors to the park today.'

'What are you three doing?' a voice
asked curiously. Evie looked up. The voice
belonged to one of the boys who had been
smashing at the puddles. His friend was
beside him. 'What's going on?' he asked
again, his arms folded in front of his chest.
They were older than Evie and the others,
taller too. But the boy's smile seemed
friendly enough.

'Nothing,' Ryan said.

'Well, that's not true,' the boy said.
'You've been staring at the ground and
walking around in circles like pigeons.
You've dropped something.'

'It's nothing,' Isabelle said.

'I don't believe you. I'm Will, this is Samir. We'll help you look,' the boy said with a grin.

'We don't need any help, thank you,' Isabelle said primly.

Evie moved closer to the balance beams – was that a horseshoe print on the ground? Oh. No. It was just the curved heel of a welly boot.

'Go on,' Will was saying, 'tell us what you've lost. Whatever it is must be important, you've been at it for ages. We were watching you.'

Evie glanced up from the task. Isabelle had folded her arms in front of her chest and was standing legs akimbo. She was in her

I-mean-business stance.

Oh-oh.

'Why don't you two go and boil your heads?' Isabelle said crossly. 'We're busy and we haven't got time to be bothered by you.'

Will folded his arms in exactly the same way as Isabelle. 'That's not very nice. I was only offering to help.'

'Well, your help is not wanted.'

'Fine.' Will lunged forward suddenly and whipped Isabelle's bobble hat right off her head.

'Hey!' she yelled angrily. But it made no difference. Will leapt away, waving Isabelle's hat like a flag. Samir laughed and chased after him. Isabelle was right on their tail,

Ryan too. They shuffled through the snow, kicking white clouds up into the frosty air.

'Give that back!' Isabelle yelled.

Evie wasn't to be distracted though. She checked her watch. They only had another fifteen minutes before they had to meet the unicorn and share any news. And Nana Em was expecting them for elevenses. So far they had nothing at all to tell Arthur. Junior was still missing, with no clues.

'Catch!' Will threw the hat to Samir, who leapt like a deer to catch it. He twirled in a circle and raced in the other direction. Ryan sidestepped awkwardly to keep up.

Evie sighed. There was a little foal somewhere nearby who was probably cold and frightened. He was lost and just wanted his parent back. And all anyone else could do was chase after a silly hat. She glared at Samir. 'Stop messing around!' she snapped.

He wasn't listening. The chase had reached the climbing frame. Samir danced in and out of the red ropes, holding Isabelle's hat high above his head. Will yelled encouragement. Isabelle and Ryan jumped to reach it. Samir threw the hat. Ryan leapt, but Will was too tall – he caught it easily.

'Isabelle,' Evie called, 'we haven't got time for this.'

'But it's my favourite hat!' Isabelle said.

'*It's my favourite hat*,' Will mimicked. He threw it back to Samir.

Samir jumped up and grabbed one of the climbing ropes with his free hand. He swung on to the climbing web. He swayed gently in the middle, like a spider. He waved the hat in the air.

Enough was enough, Evie thought. She had to get her friends back on track. They had an important job – Arthur and Junior were counting on them.

Evie looked at Samir, halfway up the climbing web, and smiled. She knew what she was going to do.

Chapter 7

Evie looked around to see if anyone was looking. The nearest family were building a snowman and weren't looking her way at all. She just had Will and Samir to worry about. She ducked behind the wooden climbing wall and reached for her bracelet. She turned it, once, twice, three times, a twist of gold magic ran up her wrist. In moments, she was invisible!

She sneaked out from behind the wall.

'You can't get me!' Samir taunted.

Isabelle and Ryan were trying to get to the base of the rope web, but Will was throwing snowballs to keep them back.

It was simple for Evie to tread carefully, trying to put her feet in old prints, and creep up on the net.

'Give it back right now, or I'll, I'll …' Isabelle was fuming with anger. There was practically smoke coming from her ears.

'You'll what?' Samir laughed. 'Tell your mum?'

Evie gripped the rope web silently and

began to climb. She had to be careful – if she set the web swaying, Samir might notice. So far, no one was looking her way.

She was inches away from him now, she'd climbed right to his side without him feeling a thing. He was holding the hat out in front of him, though. She leaned forward, slowly, slowly, gripping the rope tight in one hand and wedging her feet into the corners of their squares so that she wouldn't fall. She stretched her fingers closer and closer to his hand. He dangled the hat between his thumb and finger.

Evie made one last lunge – and plucked the hat from his hand!

'Hey! What?' Samir gasped.

Evie scampered higher up the web. She had to get out of his reach. The web shook and wobbled.

'What's going on?' Samir shouted.

Evie was at the top. She straddled the top beam and shoved the hat under her jumper.

As far as Samir could tell the hat he'd been holding moments earlier had just vanished into thin air!

'Will!' he yelled. 'Did you see that? The play park is haunted!'

Will stopped throwing snowballs. Isabelle and Ryan looked up.

'I'm telling the truth!' Samir said. 'It's haunted. The ropes just started shaking for no reason and something stole the hat. There's ghosts, I'm telling you!'

Isabelle and Ryan grinned. They'd guessed what was going on.

'Woooo ...' Evie muttered in her most ghostly voice. 'Woooo ...'

'Did you hear that?' Isabelle said.

'Woooo …'

'What is it?' Will said, his voice quaking.
'I don't like it.'

'My mum says …' Ryan said, stepping
closer to Will so that he could whisper
near his ear. 'She says that the ghost of an
old Park Warden wanders here in winter.
He's hunting children who mess around
and make trouble. And if he catches them,
they're never seen again.'

Will's knees nearly buckled in fright.
Samir climbed down, two rows at a
time, then leapt into the snow. Will helped
him up.

'Woooo …' Evie said again, for good
measure.

'Leg it!' Samir yelled to Will. They grabbed each other as they ran away from the climbing web, past the balance beams and out through the gate. Evie watched them from the top of the climbing web. They raced all the way to the lake without stopping to look back.

Then, she pulled out the hat and threw it down to Isabelle. It appeared slowly on the ground.

'Thanks! That was brilliant,' Isabelle said. She picked up the bobble hat, shook the snow off it and jammed it down on her head.

'Did you see their faces?' Ryan laughed.

'I did,' Evie said. 'But I better stop being

invisible and we need to look for Junior. We've lost too much time.'

'Well, don't appear up there,' Ryan said. 'Everyone in the park will be able to see you.'

She was about to swing her leg back and begin to climb down, when she froze. If everyone in the park could see the top of the climbing web, then the top of the web could see the whole park! She had an amazing view! 'You two,' she shouted down to the ground. 'Get up here quickly, see if you can see any sign of Junior.'

Ryan and Isabelle scrambled up, eager to help.

Evie scanned the park carefully. They

86

could see the main hill where sledgers
trundled down. She thought she could just
make out Nana Em still sliding in delight.
There was the small café, near the hill.
Further to the right was the lake, looking
cold and dark. Then to the right of that
were the woods. The trees there were older
and taller than the little copse by the gate.

87

She looked and looked, but there was no sign of Junior.

Evie sighed. 'Our time's nearly up. We should go and tell the unicorn that we haven't found him.'

'Wait,' Ryan said. 'Look! What's that?'

He pointed towards the woods and the dark tangle of trees. There was something glittering on a low branch.

'It's just the sun reflecting on snow,' Isabelle said. She started to climb down.

'No,' Ryan said, 'it isn't. It's magic! It's gold magic.'

There were splashes of magic all over the park, where people played or laughed together. But this was a bright gold thread all on its own. There was nothing and no one nearby that might have made it.

Evie tingled and gripped the bar tighter. 'Do you think Junior made it? Unicorns are full of magic.'

'Yes,' Ryan said. 'It's worth taking a look, isn't it? I mean, it's the best lead we've found, so far.'

Evie climbed down, with the others right behind. Just then, the clock on the distance church tower chimed the half hour. Time was up.

'We have to go and meet Arthur,' Evie said. It would be terrible if they didn't go back to the meeting place. The unicorn would think they didn't care, or hadn't

bothered looking at all!

'We'll split up,' Isabelle said. 'Me and Ryan will meet Arthur. You go and see if that really is a clue to finding Junior.'

Evie nodded firmly. It was a plan. Then she raced towards the speck of gold in the dark woods.

Chapter 8

Evie ran as fast as she could to reach the
wisp of gold. She dipped her head and let
her arms swing her body into the run. She
had to see if Junior was in the woods and
then get the news back to his dad as quickly
as possible. Puffs of snow kicked up behind
her as she went.

Yes! It was definitely magic. Gold light twisted like tinsel around the low-lying branch of a pine tree. She could see clearly now, something had pushed its way through, one or two twigs had snapped in half. Had it been Junior?

'Junior? Are you here?' She called his name softly into the shadows.

Evie reached up and pushed aside the snapped branch. The soft snow on the ground gave way to layers of dropped pine needles. Her footprints didn't crunch any more, they were like the soft pad of a cat. The air smelled of damp leaves. The sounds of the park were muffled by the bushes – everyone seemed very far away.

Evie shivered.

'Junior,' she called, a little louder.

She crept further into the woods. There was no path to speak of, she had to wind in and out of the trees to make her way through the tangle of boughs.

Crack!

Something snapped behind her. She spun around. But there was no one there. It's just a fox, or a squirrel, she told herself.

Something rustled in a bush nearby.

Then a squawk came from overhead.

Her heart thumped in her chest.

Perhaps it was best to be invisible? The wood was a bit scarier by herself than she wanted. She twisted her bracelet, one, twice, three times and saw her arm, then the rest of her, fade and fade until she couldn't see herself at all.

Phew. That was better. Now she'd be the one doing the sneaking up, not the beasties in the bushes!

She had been walking for a few minutes when she realised she could hear something besides the rustle and caws of the animals in the wood.

Someone was crying. It was soft and sad and gentle, but it was definitely there, right at the edge of her hearing.

'Hello?' she called. 'Junior? Is that you?'

'Hello?' a little whimpering voice called back.

'Don't worry, I'm coming to find
you!' Evie said, in the bravest voice she
could muster.

'Who's there?' the quiet little voice
said again.

Evie headed towards it. The trees
thinned out until she was standing in a
small clearing. There, in the middle of the

clearing, was a tiny unicorn, no taller than her waist. His head hung low, his stubby little horn pointed towards the ground. His legs were shivering in the cold.

'Junior!' Evie said softly.

Junior's head rose slowly, but he didn't move. He bleated sadly. As she stepped closer, Evie realised why he was still. A fence ran through the clearing, three lines of barbed wire strung between wooden posts. One of the posts had fallen flat and Junior must have stepped over it without seeing, because his back leg was twisted in the wire. He was trapped!

'Oh, Junior,' she whispered.

'Who's there?' Junior's dark eyes were

wide and frightened. He cowered away
from her voice.

Of course! She was still invisible. He had
no idea where her voice was coming from.
Evie twisted her bracelet three times and
slowly she appeared beside the unicorn.

He snorted in alarm.

'It's OK,' she said. 'It's OK. I'm going to
help. Can you stay still, please? I'm going to
take a look.'

She rested a hand on Junior's neck,
stroking and soothing him until he wasn't
shivering quite so much. Then, with one
hand resting on his body, so that he knew
exactly where she was, she moved to take a
look at his leg.

Ouch. She couldn't help but wince. The wire was wrapped tight around his right leg, just above his silver-tipped hoof. The silvery fur on his fetlock was stained with red drips of blood. She could feel him shake and quiver under her palm.

'Hush. It will be OK,' Evie said. She thought about all the times that Mum had

nursed their scrapes and scratches. Mum
always spoke with a smile in her voice,
just to show that there was no reason to be
worried.

Evie did her best to copy Mum's voice.
But she was worried. The barbs of wire
had cut into Junior's skin. The more he'd
pulled to try to free himself, the tighter
it gripped.

She, very, very gently, touched Junior's leg.

He squealed and stumbled away from her.
The wire kept him from moving far, but a
fresh cut appeared on his fetlock. 'Hush,
hush, there, you're all right. I won't hurt
you,' Evie said.

But it would hurt. She knew it would.

There was no way of untangling him without hurting him. She felt her own lip tremble. She wished she knew what to do.

'I want my daddy,' Junior whinnied. 'I lost my daddy.'

Of course. That's what was needed! Junior's dad. He could talk to Junior and soothe him, while she and the others worked together to free his leg.

'Junior, I'm going to go away but only for a minute,' she told him.

'No!' Junior gasped. 'Don't leave me on my own again.'

'It's OK. I know where your daddy is, I'm going to go and fetch him. Would you like that?'

Junior's eyes glistened with tears.

'I need you to be brave, just for a little bit longer. Can you do that?'

Junior blinked a few times, his eyes fixed on Evie. Then, he nodded. 'I can. Yes. But please ... hurry.'

She stood, as if to attention, and nodded back. She was going to run as if she had wings!

Evie turned back the way she came and launched herself through the trees, battling the branches and twigs aside.

Soon she burst out of the woods on to the crunchy snow. Her breath came in gasps, she could feel her pulse pounding in her ears. But she had to find Arthur. Junior was cold and frightened and in pain. He needed his daddy.

So, Evie was going to get him.

Chapter 9

Evie ran as fast as she could across the park, she streamed past the adventure playground, headed, like an arrow, to the copse of trees by the gate.

As she got closer, she saw Ryan and Isabelle coming out with the unicorn walking tall behind them.

Even from this distance, she could tell that Arthur was still frightened. His nostrils flared and the muscles on his flank rippled with energy. She had to get to him and tell him she'd found Junior.

Evie put on one last urgent sprint.

'I've found him, I've found him – but he's trapped,' she gasped.

'Where?' Arthur demanded.

'Follow me, this way!' Evie turned on her heels and raced back the way she'd come. Beside her, the unicorn's hooves crushed the snow, sending sparkling clouds of ice into the air around him. It was so strange that no one else in the park could see him. They tore past people playing, the sound of laughter and games, the smell of hot chocolate and tea being sipped, and no one even looked their way. The unicorn was completely invisible.

Evie thought about Junior, alone and scared. 'Come on!' she urged the others. Ryan and Isabelle raced along too.

Soon, they were back at the place where the tiny trace of gold magic clung to the branch. 'This way!'

They all plunged into the darkness of the trees. It was less scary now that she was with her friends. Evie led the way to the clearing, where Junior whickered with joy as they burst through the trees. 'Daddy!' he cried.

'Junior. Oh, Junior, I've been so worried.' Arthur ducked his head so that he was nose to nose with Junior. They butted in gentle delight at being reunited. Evie felt herself smiling, and, when she looked over to Isabelle and Ryan, they both had huge grins spread across their faces.

Until Isabelle looked down and saw how Junior's leg was bleeding. 'Poor thing,' she said. 'We have to help him.'

Evie thought about Mum. She was going to be working, on Christmas Day, to help people who were hurt and sick and frightened. Evie was going to have to be just like Mum now, if Junior was going to be free.

107

'Right, everyone,' Evie said. 'We need to work together. Mr Prancing Proudfoot, eh ...' She couldn't remember the unicorn's very fancy name.

'My friends call me Arthur,' the unicorn said gruffly. 'Thank you for finding Junior.'

'Arthur. Please could you stay close to Junior? He needs you to help him be brave. Ryan and Isabelle and I are going to work to untangle him from the wire. We'll do our best, but it might hurt.'

Arthur stood right next to Junior, his head close to his son's, so that Junior could lean against him. Evie and Isabelle crouched next to the twist of wire. Ryan steadied Junior.

Evie flexed her fingers a few times – she

couldn't let her hands shake – then reached

out to grip the wire. She soon saw that

the wire had snapped away from the fence

post and was curled around Junior's leg.

She eased the loose end away from Junior.

She heard him hiss in pain, but leaning

against his dad gave him courage and he

stayed stock-still. She passed the length of wire to Isabelle who was ready on the other side of Junior's leg. Isabelle unwound the wire on her side. They worked quickly, passing the sharp wire back and forth between them until it was all unwound.

Junior leapt up in joy. 'Thank you!' he said.

'Be careful,' Evie said, 'you need to clean the cut or it might get infected.' That was the sort of thing Mum said all the time.

'She's right,' Arthur said. 'We need to get you straight home.' Arthur dropped his head gently over Junior's, pulling him into a hug. Then he looked at Evie. 'I can't thank you enough. Is there anything we can do for you?'

Evie sighed. The only thing she wanted was for her family to be together at Christmas, but she knew she couldn't have that. It was her own fault for making such a fuss about the bike. 'It's all right,' she said. 'I'm just pleased we could help.'

'What?' Isabelle asked in disbelief. 'You don't want to ask for a ride on a unicorn's back, or for your magic bracelets to last for longer than three days? Or for the snow to turn to marshmallow?'

Evie laughed and slipped her hand through Isabelle's. 'No. Sometimes it's enough just to do the right thing.'

'You're weird,' Isabelle said with a grin.

'Come on, Junior, say goodbye,' Arthur said.

'I hope we see you again! Goodbye and thank you,' Junior said eagerly. Then the two unicorns stepped towards the shadows of the trees and were gone, as if by magic.

All that was left were a few hoofprints on the ground and a tangle of broken fencing.

'Well,' Ryan said, 'I never expected to free a unicorn this morning. I thought we'd just do a bit of sledging, perhaps make a snowman.'

Sledging! Cripes! Nana Em and Grandpa would be wondering where she'd got to. They'd been away for ages. 'We'd better get back,' Evie said.

As they walked out of the woods, Evie
glanced back at the clearing and the barbed
wire. It was dangerous to leave it there.
Someone else might get tangled and hurt.
She knew just the person they needed to tell.

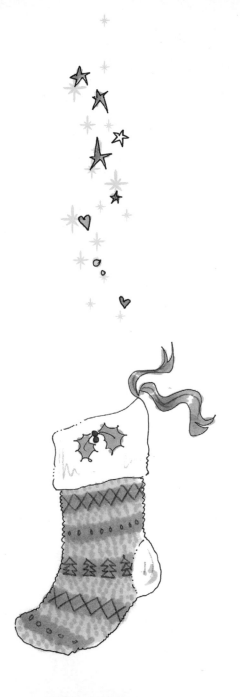

Chapter 10

Nana Em and Grandpa were sitting at the
little café at the bottom of the slope when
Evie and the others made their way back.
Lily hadn't quite sledged enough, so she was
still hurtling up and down the hill.

'There you are!' Nana Em said in delight.
'We were going to send out a search party.'

'Sorry, Nana Em, we got a bit caught up.'
Evie caught Isabelle's eye and they both
giggled. She dropped into a plastic chair
beside Grandpa. 'We were exploring,' she
told him.

'Did you find anything good?' he asked.
'Sometimes there's lovely wildlife in this

park. You wouldn't expect it in the middle of the city, but there are bats and foxes and all sorts.'

'We didn't see any bats,' Evie said. 'But we did find a fence with barbed wire and a broken post. It was really dangerous.'

Ryan leaned on the arm of her chair. 'An animal could easily get hurt on it,' he added.

Grandpa frowned. 'I don't like the sound of that,' he said.

'I was wondering if we could call Dad and ask him to come and fix it?' Evie asked.

'That sounds champion,' Grandpa agreed. He took out his phone and made a quick call. Evie could hear Dad's voice at the other end, though she wasn't sure what he said.

But when Grandpa hung up and smiled at her, she knew Dad was on his way.

There was enough time for everyone to have one more go on the sledge, whizzing down the hill with the sharp wind on their faces and grins as wide as a river, before Dad arrived.

He was carrying his toolbox, bundled up against the cold.

'Dad!' Lily launched herself at Dad and wrapped her arms around his legs. He wobbled in the snow, but stayed upright.

'Hi, Dad,' Evie said. It had only been a few hours since she'd seen him, but she felt really happy that he was there with them all. She reached up and gave him a hug too.

'What's that in aid of?' he said, obviously pleased – a sprinkle of gold magic showered above him.

'Nothing. It's just nice to have you in the park, that's all.'

'Why don't you show your dad where the barbed wire is?' Nana Em said. 'There'll be a hot chocolate waiting here for you both when you get back.' Isabelle and Ryan stayed with Nana Em – they'd not had enough sledging quite yet!

Evie leaned against Dad as they walked together, side-by-side towards the wood. The sounds of the sledgers drifted back and the snow crunched sharply beneath their feet.

'You're quiet,' Dad said. 'Everything OK?'

'Hmm,' Evie said. She was thinking how nice it was to have Dad with them, and she wished Mum could be too. She wished it could be all of them together always.

'It will be great to come here in spring, won't it?' Dad said. 'Who knows, if you're really lucky you might even have a new bike to race around on.'

They were at the edge of the wood. The gold wisp of magic that the unicorn had left had faded; now it looked more like a small patch of sunshine on bark.

'Won't that be good?' Dad asked.

'What?' Evie hadn't been concentrating.

'Riding your new bike. If you get one, that is,' Dad added quickly.

Evie had to say something. She had to.
'About that.' She looked down. The ground
was covered in dried, old leaves and spiky
needles.

'Yes?' Dad asked.

'I think a new bike would be lovely. And
if I do get one, that's brilliant. But you know
more than anything, I just want everyone
to be happy and be together. I didn't mean
for anyone to think a bike was the most
important thing. Not ever.' The words came
out like a flurry of snowflakes, tumbling
over each other in a rush.

Dad laughed. 'Evie, slow down, you aren't
making any sense.'

Evie didn't think she could say it all again.

She tugged her coat around herself and jammed her hands in her pockets.

They reached the clearing. With Dad here the shadows didn't seem as scary as before. But the barbed wire was still curled in a tight spring on the floor.

'Oh yes,' Dad said, 'this is nasty. You were right to get Grandpa to call me. But we'll have it sorted in just a minute.'

Dad lifted the fallen fence post. 'I'll need the mallet,' he said.

Evie opened his toolbox and took out the mallet.

As Dad hit the post back into the ground with three solid whacks of the mallet, Evie put the mallet back and passed Dad his staple gun, like a nurse assisting in an operation.

Dad looked at her quizzically. 'Evie, you look so glum. Why don't you tell me what's on your mind?'

Evie sighed and crouched near the ground. She picked up fallen acorn cups and began balancing them on top of each other. 'I heard you and Mum talking,' she said. 'Sorry for listening. But I heard Mum say she won't be home at Christmas.'

'Oh,' Dad said.

'And you told her to think of the money. And the only reason we need to worry about money is because I've been nagging for a bike for weeks and weeks.'

123

Dad gave the fence post a little shake. It was firmly in the ground. 'Evie, love, I'm sorry you heard the news that way. But that's not it at all. Mum working has got nothing to do with you nagging.'

Dad put down the staple gun and came to sit next to Evie on the ground.

'You'll get wet,' she warned.

'It doesn't matter.' He dropped his arm around her shoulder and pulled her into a hug. 'Your mum takes her job very seriously indeed, you know that, don't you?'

Evie knew. She'd tried to copy Mum when she helped Junior because she knew what a good nurse Mum was.

'Mum cares about the people she looks

after, and that doesn't stop on Christmas Day. I only said think of the money to make her laugh. It's the last thing she thinks about while she's doing her job.'

Evie leaned against Dad's shoulder. 'So, it wasn't for the bike?'

'No, silly. Who's to say you're even getting a bike!' Dad laughed. 'Now, why don't you help me mend this fence, hey?'

He picked up the staple gun. Evie lifted the loose barbed wire and passed the end to Dad. With a few pings the wire was back in place.

'Thanks, Dad,' Evie said.

'You're welcome. But maybe don't tell your mum I let you touch barbed wire.

She'd have kittens!'

'But we've made it safe, we did a good job,' Evie said.

Dad dropped his arm around her shoulder. 'We did, didn't we?' He closed his toolbox and picked it up. 'I've been thinking. How would it be, do you think, if we had Christmas a bit early, this year? We could pretend that Christmas Eve is Christmas Day. That way Mum could be with us.'

'Really?' Evie felt a rush of happiness at the idea. Christmas come early!

'Yes,' Dad said. 'If I'm quick, I can write to Father Christmas and see what he thinks.'

'Hurray! Yes! Yes, please!' Evie leapt through the trees and out into the sparkling

snow. She danced into the frosty air and
waved at the sledging hill, hoping the others
would see her. She had brilliant news –
Christmas was only two sleeps away now.

And she felt that perhaps Arthur had
given her a wish, after all.

Enjoyed this story?

Find out how Evie's
adventures began in

The Silver Unicorn

Chapter 1

'Evie!' Mum called up the stairs. 'We'll be heading out in fifteen minutes, are you set?'

Evie Hall was sitting on the end of her tidily made bed. She was staring at her carefully laced school shoes – and she was totally panicking.

What if her new school was full of bullies

and monsters? What if the teachers were meaner than a crocodile with a cold? What if all the other pupils ignored her?

Worse. What if they noticed her?

Her heart thumped like a brass band in a washing machine.

'Evie! Are you listening, love?'

She had to be brave. She had to pick up her book bag and stand up. Even though her legs felt like they'd turned to warm plasticine. There was no way she could just stay on her bed for the whole day, however much she wanted to. She had already double- and triple- checked that she had her pencil case and Nana Em's phone number in case of emergencies. She was set. Except for the plasticine leg problem, of course.

Luna, Evie's silver-grey cat, meowed loudly, and leapt on to her lap. Her claws dug like needles, prodding Evie to move.

'Ow! OK, OK, I'm going,' Evie said.

Luna gave a happy purr and stepped on to the bed, where she promptly curled up into a ball. She clearly considered her job done.

'It's all right for you,' Evie said. 'You can spend all day snoozing, you don't have to start at a new school.'

Luna shut her eyes. Snoozing was her favourite.

Evie picked up her book bag and tramped downstairs.

Mum was in the hall, pulling a brush

through her hair. Evie could hear Dad trying to get her little sister Lily to eat-her-breakfast-not-play-with-it. Lily was mithering as usual.

There were still cardboard boxes piled beside the front door. They hadn't been unpacked from the move.

Evie was about to ask Mum one last time whether she really, really, really had to change schools, just because they'd moved house, and her old school was miles away, and they-had-been-through-this-already, when the doorbell rang.

The postman stood on the doorstep. 'Welcome to Javelin Street!' he said cheerfully, as he handed a parcel to Mum.

'Thanks!' Mum replied brightly. 'We love it here, don't we, Evie?'

Evie said nothing. She *liked* it here, because they were much closer to Nana Em and Grandpa – next door, in fact. And she had her own room in the attic and didn't have to share with Lily. Which was good because Lily was annoying: she was five and thought the sky was blue because it had rain in it. But *liking* it here wasn't at all the same thing as *loving* it – the one huge, ginormous thing it was missing was her old friends.

'Oh!' Mum looked at the wrapper on the parcel. 'It's for you, Evie.'

For her? She never got parcels. Except on her birthday, which wasn't for ages.

Her tummy did an excited flip, instead of a terrified one. She took the parcel from Mum and cradled it curiously. What was it? Who was it from?

Mum was still chatting to the postman, so Evie slipped into the front room. It was the good room, with the red settee that Myla the dog wasn't allowed to sit on and shed her fur all over. She wanted somewhere quiet – which meant away from Lily – to open the parcel.

It was square, and fitted comfortably between her palms. Pink wrapping paper was held in place with jewel-coloured blue and green ribbons. Her name was written in looped handwriting across the

front. Handwriting that Evie recognised –
Grandma Iris! She lived a long way away
in Jamaica, but she often wrote letters and
cards to her grand-daughters. Today she had
sent something really special.

Evie tugged the ribbon free and let the
paper fall. Inside was a box, made of white
card with a red lid. She lifted the lid, her
fingers tingling with excitement.

There, nestled inside soft tissue paper, was
a bracelet. Evie's breath caught. Grandma
Iris had sent her a present, just when she
needed it. She lifted it out carefully. The
bracelet twinkled in the dust motes that
danced in shining sunlight. Tightly plaited
silks criss-crossed in colourful streams.

There were beads too, exactly the same silvery-grey colour as Luna's fur. It was beautiful. Evie noticed a small card resting on top of the tissue paper, written by Grandma Iris, 'Good luck at your new school,' it said. 'Have a magical time!'

Magical? School? Ha! There was more chance of pigs putting on an acrobatic aerial show than of having a magical time on her first day. Still, Evie felt warm knowing that Grandma Iris was thinking of her.

She slipped the bracelet on – it fitted perfectly, as though it had been made just for her. For a second, Evie could almost feel Grandma Iris' arms around her in a tight hug. The sun seemed to shine more brightly

through the lace curtains. She felt a tear
in her eye, and the sunbeam shattered into
kaleidoscope shards of gold sparkles.

'Evie,' Mum stuck her head into the room,
'I'll walk you and Lily there. All set?'

Evie blinked and pulled her sleeve down quickly. She knew Mum wouldn't let her wear jewellery to school, but she wanted to keep the warm feeling with her for as long as she could. She pushed the bracelet high up her arm.

Myla bounded into the room. She was

panting and her tongue lolled. It looked exactly like a big grin. She woofed excitedly.

'Myla wants to walk with us,' Evie said, sure that she was right.

Mum laughed. 'Does she now? Well, I'm not stopping every thirty seconds to sniff lamp-posts. We're in a rush! Perhaps tomorrow, Myla.'

Myla stopped grinning. She looked the way Lily did when she got mardy and stuck out her bottom lip.

'Sorry, Myla,' Evie said. She patted the dog's head. 'But what Mum says goes.'

'That's right,' Mum agreed. 'And this mum says it's time for you to start your new school. Let's go.'

Evie and friends

Evie

Full name: Evie Hall

Lives in: Sheffield

Family: Mum, Dad, younger sister Lily

Pets: Chocolate Labrador Myla and cat Luna

Favourite foods: rice, peas and chicken – lasagna – and chocolate bourbon biscuits!

Best thing about Evie: friendly and determined!

Isabelle

Full name: Isabelle Carter

Lives in: Sheffield

Family: Mum, Dad, older sister Lizzie

Favourite foods: sweet treats – and anything spicy!

Best thing about Isabelle: she's the life and soul of the party!

Ryan

Full name: Ryan Harris

Lives in: Sheffield

Family: lives with his mum, visits his dad

Pets: would love a dog …

Favourite foods: Marmite, chocolate – and anything with pasta!

Best thing about Ryan: easy-going, and fun to be with!

Evie's Magic Bracelet

★ ★ ♡ ☆ ♥ Christmas

Find your perfect activity for when it snows!

What's your favourite item of winter clothing?

A. ❏ Scarf.
B. ❏ Gloves.
C. ❏ Woolly hat.

What's the best winter animal?

A. ❏ Penguin.
B. ❏ Polar bear.
C. ❏ Robin.

The best thing about snow is ...

A. ❏ Snowflakes!
B. ❏ The cold.
C. ❏ Seeing a new white landscape.

The most important feature of a snowman is ...

A. ☐ Its hat.
B. ☐ A carrot nose.
C. ☐ Its smile!

I'm best at ...

A. ☐ Using my imagination.
B. ☐ Throwing.
C. ☐ Running.

Which character do you relate to the most?

A. ☐ Isabelle.
B. ☐ Evie.
C. ☐ Ryan.

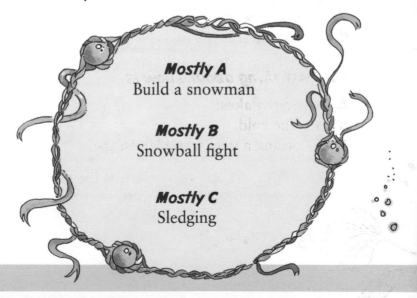

Mostly A
Build a snowman

Mostly B
Snowball fight

Mostly C
Sledging

Step-by-step snowflakes

Make the perfect winter decoration
with these super fun and individual snowflakes!

You will need:

- A square sheet of paper (white looks like snow, but any colour will do!)
- Scissors (ask an adult)

Instructions:

Step 1 – Start with your square piece of paper. Fold it diagonally in half to make a triangle.

Step 2 – Fold this triangle in half along the middle to make an even smaller triangle.

Step 3 – Imagine this triangle divided into equal thirds (you can mark them on with a pencil if it's easier!). Fold one corner across the middle to make two thirds. Do the same with the other side too.

Step 4 – Flip the paper to the other side. You should see a triangle with two points sticking out of the bottom. Use your scissors to cut off these points.

Step 5 – Get your scissors and cut shapes into the remaining triangle – they can be any shape or size, so feel free to use your imagination! Just make sure not to cut the whole way through!

Step 6 – Open up your triangle and see your snowflake!

Paper snowflakes look great as they are – but you can always customise them more with stickers, drawing, or even glitter!

Can you find all the words?

BRACELET	MAGIC
EVIE	SLEDGE
ISABELLE	UNICORN
RYAN	SNOW
FRIENDS	FOAL

U	T	G	C	C	J	F	A	U	B
N	T	R	I	S	O	J	I	X	R
C	R	G	Y	A	T	S	H	G	A
C	A	O	L	A	A	C	E	H	C
M	I	V	C	B	N	G	G	G	E
S	D	N	E	I	R	F	D	S	L
P	V	L	Y	B	N	J	E	N	E
A	L	E	V	I	E	U	L	O	T
E	C	Q	D	S	K	V	S	W	F
S	Y	A	O	Z	G	S	V	M	I
J	R	W	J	N	K	E	D	I	T

Wordsearch answers:

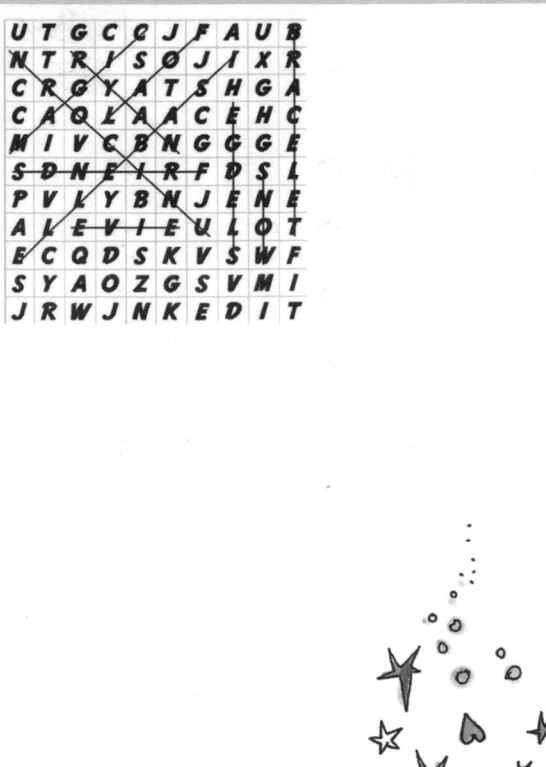

Evie's winter facts

- 💜 No two snowflakes have the same pattern – each one is unique!

- 💜 Snow is actually colourless – it only looks white because light is reflected off it.

- 💜 The coldest recorded temperature in the UK was –27.5°C in Scotland!

- 💜 Polar bears have black skin! It helps them absorb the heat in cold temperatures.

Jessica Ennis-Hill grew up in Sheffield with her parents and younger sister. She has been World and European heptathlon champion and won gold at the London 2012 Olympics and silver at Rio 2016. She still lives in Sheffield and enjoys reading stories to her son every night.

You can find Jessica on Twitter **@J_Ennis**, on Facebook, and on Instagram **@jessicaennishill**

Jessica says: *'I have so many great memories of being a kid. My friends and I spent lots of time exploring and having adventures where my imagination used to run riot! It has been so much fun working with Elen Caldecott to go back to that world of stories and imagination. I hope you'll enjoy them too!'*

Elen Caldecott co-wrote the Evie's Magic Bracelet stories with Jessica. Elen lives in Totterdown, in Bristol – chosen mainly because of the cute name. She has written several warm, funny books about ordinary children doing extraordinary things.

You can find out more at www.elencaldecott.com